MEGAN
MEGAN
MEGAN
MEGAN
MEGAN
MEGAN
MEGAN
MEGAN
MEGAN
MEGAN
MEGAN

A Day at Damp Camp

by George Ella Lyon ▪ pictures by Peter Catalanotto

ORCHARD BOOKS ▪ NEW YORK

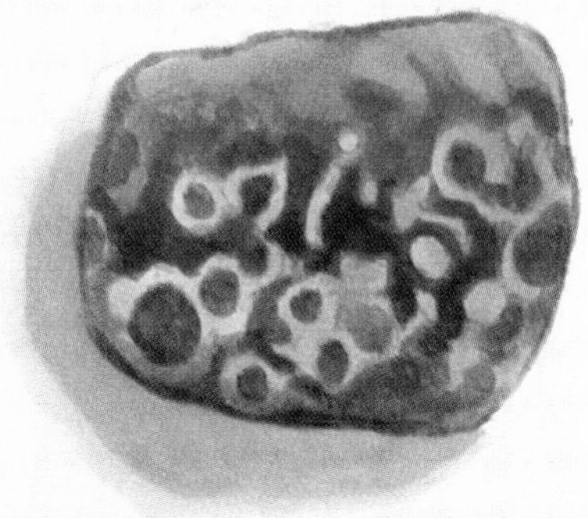

For all who love
Camp O'Cumberlands
—G.E.L.

To Yumi and Tony
—P.C.

Thanks to Helen, Melinda, Carissa, Laura, Emily, Tara, Ellen, and Kathryn
—P.C.

Orchard Books, 95 Madison Avenue, New York, NY 10016

Manufactured in the United States of America. Printed by Barton Press, Inc. Bound by Horowitz/Rae.
The text of this book is set in 33 point Mixage Black.
The illustrations are watercolor paintings reproduced in full color.

10 9 8 7 6 5 4 3 2 1

Library of Congress Cataloging-in-Publication Data
Lyon, George Ella, date. A day at damp camp / by George Ella Lyon ; pictures by Peter Catalanotto.
p. cm. "A Richard Jackson book"—Half t.p. Summary: One friend helps another through the pitfalls and pratfalls of a day at summer camp. ISBN 0-531-09504-5.—ISBN 0-531-08854-5 (lib. bdg.)
[1. Camps—Fiction. 2. Stories in rhyme.] I. Catalanotto, Peter, ill. II. Title.
PZ8.3.L9893Day 1996 [E]—dc20 95-20848

GIRLS

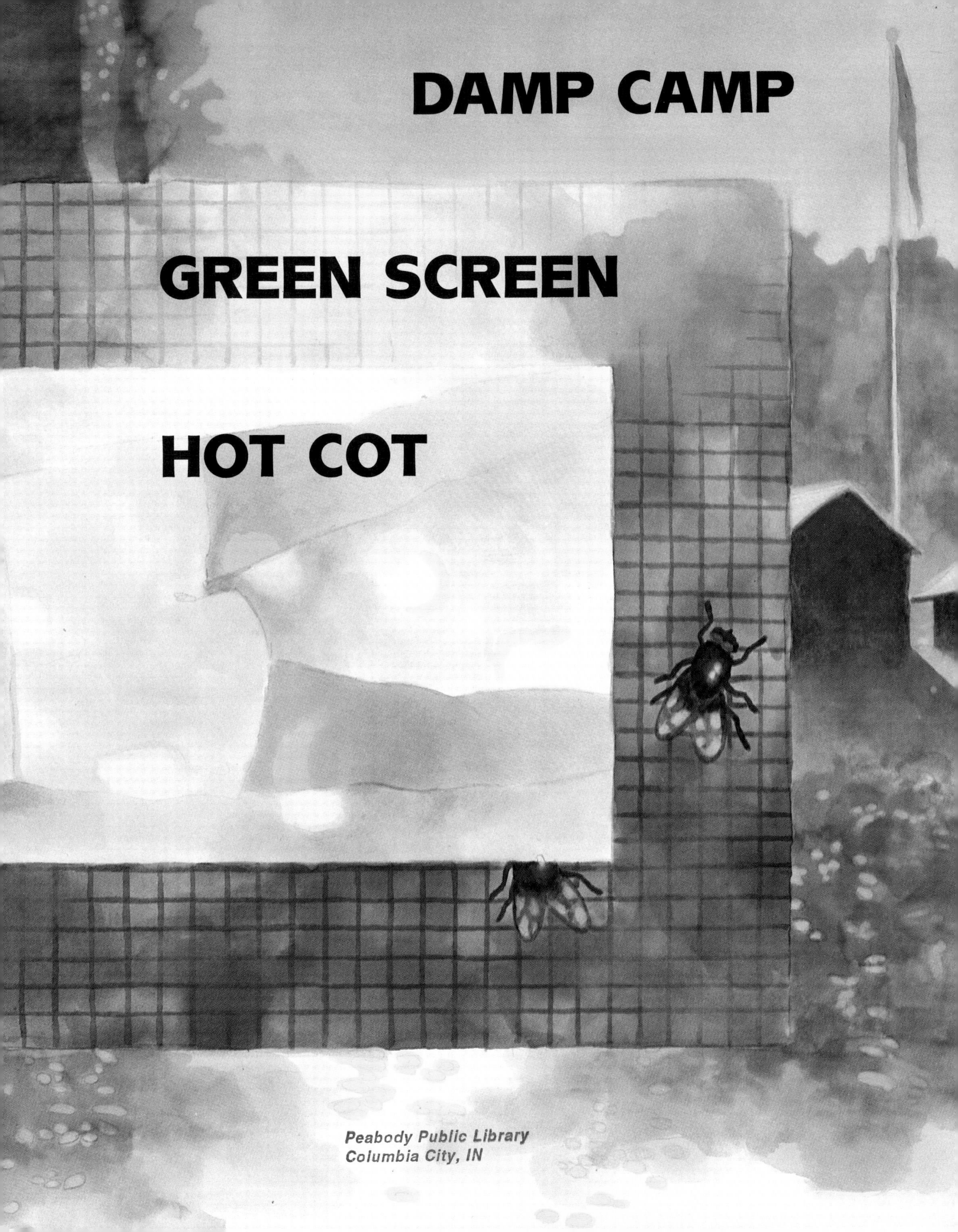

DAMP CAMP

GREEN SCREEN

HOT COT

FROG LOG

BUG TUG

SNAKE SHAKE

SEED BEAD

CRAFT RAFT

FLOAT BOAT

COOL POOL

DIVE IN
LIVE SKIN

HIGH SKY
BACK PACK
SNAIL TRAIL

SEEK CREEK

MUD FLOOD

WADE SHADE

POLE HOLE

BENT TENT

WALL FALL

BRIER FIRE

BEAN SCENE

OWN STONE

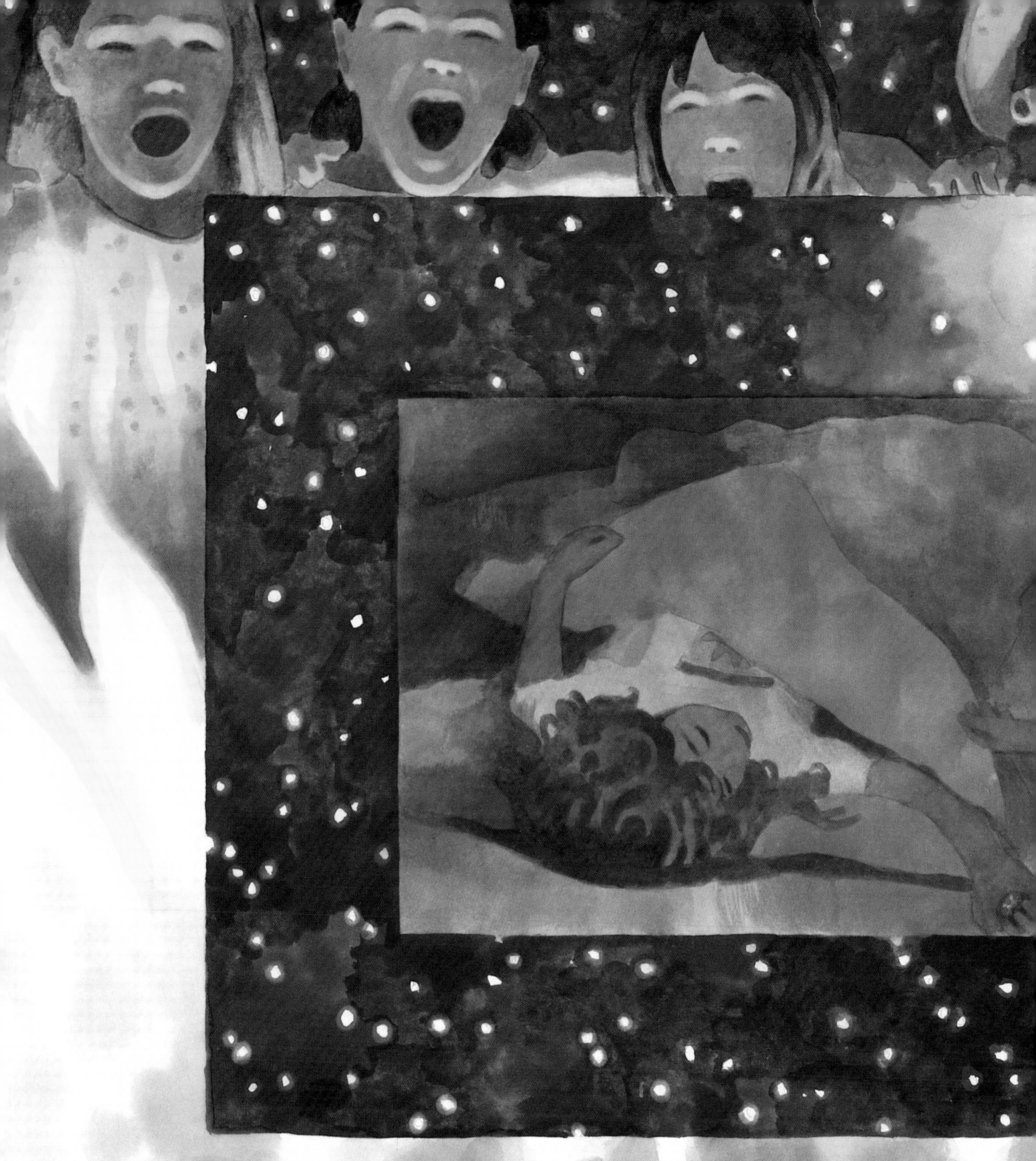

LONG SONG

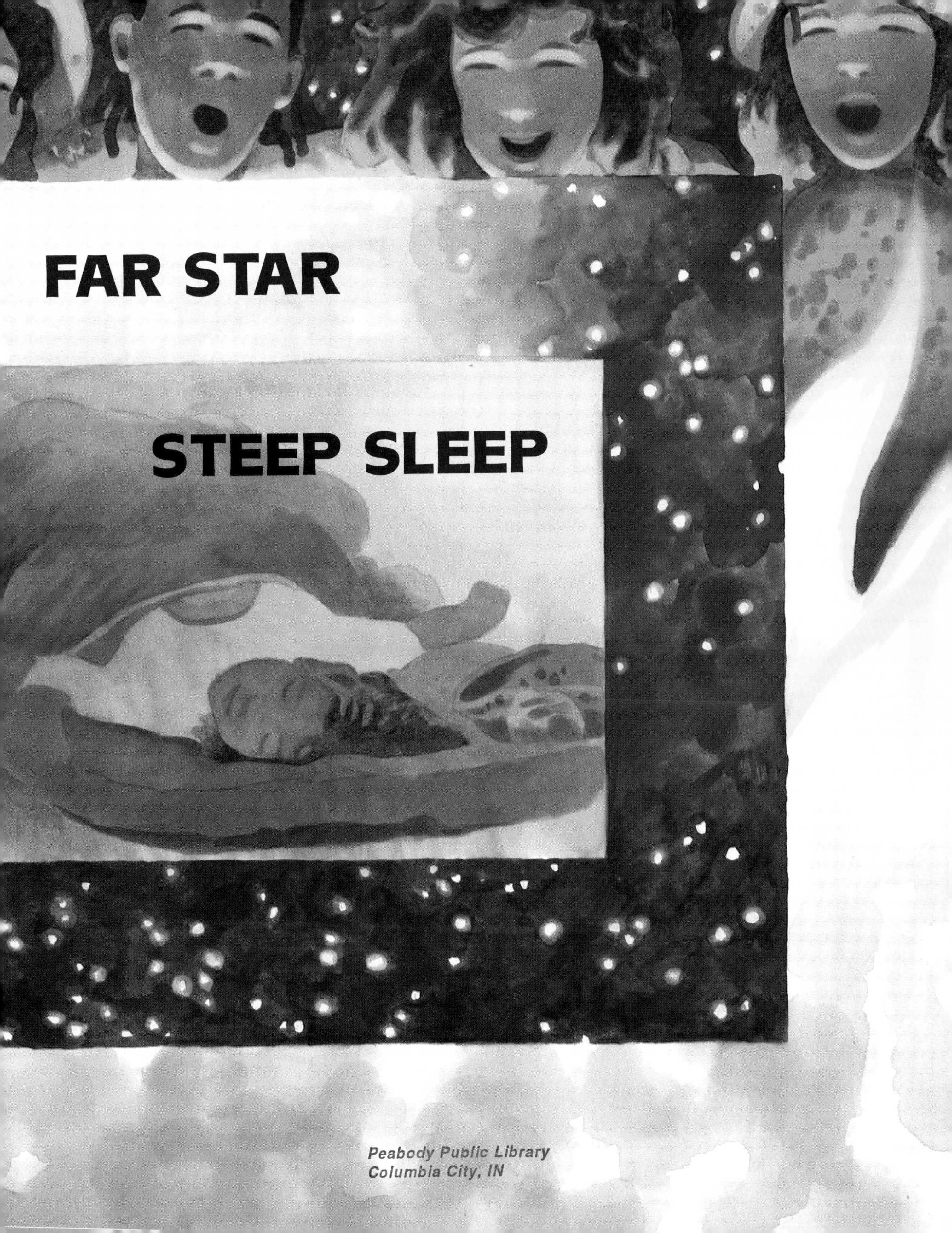

FAR STAR

STEEP SLEEP

MEGAN
MEGAN
MEGAN
MEGAN
MEG
MEG